# The Party Diaries

## Starry Henna Night

written by
Mitali Banerjee Ruths

art by
Aaliya Jaleel

BRANCHES
SCHOLASTIC INC.

For Lily, Prosun, and Navin
& Melissa, Justin, and Piper—MBR

For Reem, Sarah, Hafsa, Mus, and Mahir—AJ

Text copyright © 2023 by Mitali Banerjee Ruths
Art copyright © 2023 by Aaliya Jaleel

All rights reserved. Published by Scholastic Inc., *Publishers since 1920.* SCHOLASTIC,
BRANCHES, and associated logos are trademarks and/or registered trademarks of Scholastic Inc.

The publisher does not have any control over and does not assume any
responsibility for author or third-party websites or their content.

No part of this publication may be reproduced, stored in a retrieval system, or transmitted in any form
or by any means, electronic, mechanical, photocopying, recording, or otherwise, without written
permission of the publisher. For information regarding permission, write to Scholastic Inc., Attention:
Permissions Department, 557 Broadway, New York, NY 10012.

This book is a work of fiction. Names, characters, places, and incidents are either the product of the
author's imagination or are used fictitiously, and any resemblance to actual persons, living or dead,
business establishments, events, or locales is entirely coincidental.

Library of Congress Cataloging-in-Publication Data
Names: Ruths, Mitali Banerjee, author. | Jaleel, Aaliya, illustrator.
Title: Starry henna night / written by Mitali Banerjee Ruths ; illustrated by Aaliya Jaleel.
Description: First edition. | New York, NY : Scholastic, Inc., 2023. |
Series: The party diaries ; 2 | Audience: Ages 5–7. | Audience: Grades K–2. | Summary: When
eight-year-old Priya is hired to do a henna night for a teenage party, she and her friend Melissa are
worried their ideas might be too babyish for the older guests.
Identifiers: LCCN 2021060366 (print) | ISBN 9781338799811 (paperback) |
ISBN 9781338799828 (library binding)
Subjects: CYAC: Parties—Fiction. | East Indian Americans—Fiction. |
LCGFT: Fiction.
Classification: LCC PZ7.1.R9 St 2023 (print) | DDC
[Fic]—dc23
LC record available at https://lccn.loc.gov/2021060366

10 9 8 7 6 5 4 3 2 1          23 24 25 26 27

Printed in China          62
First edition, April 2023

Edited by Katie Carella
Book design by Maria Mercado

# TABLE OF CONTENTS

# VIP LIST
(Very Important People)

**Priya**
(Me!)

**Samir**
(My little brother, also known as Sammy)

**Baba**
(My dad, also known as Ashok)

**Dida**
(My grandmother is my mom's mom)

**Ma**
(My mom, also known as Reeta)

**My friends!**

**Ethan**
(An annoying boy in my class)

**Melissa**

**Dola**

**My mom's friends!**

**Layla Aunty**

**Padma Aunty**

**Susan Aunty**

**Neda Aunty**

(Really awesome henna artists!)

**Tara**
(Layla Aunty's niece)

# MY BUSINESS

## Monday

Hello, world! It's Priya.

I started my own business called Priya's Parties. I organize awesome parties to help endangered animals so they don't disappear forever.

My first party raised money for quokkas!

Guess what? I have another party to plan, but I can't tell you much yet.

## THINGS I <u>HAVE</u> TO DO

Empty junk from my backpack.

Finish math homework.

Read Sammy a book.

Every day this week, my little brother has picked the SAME book about dinosaurs.

# THINGS I WANT TO DO

Plan my next awesome party.

Help endangered animals.

Hang out with Melissa.

She lives next door and has a pet iguana.

Harry

I'm still new to the whole party-planning business. My first job was planning a birthday party for Layla Aunty.

DIY decorations
(Do-It-Yourself)

Me!

orange theme

Layla Aunty

HAPPY BIRTHDAY LAYLA AUNTY

This party helped quokkas!

Layla Aunty's niece, Tara, saw the pictures on my social media. She asked if I could plan a party for her.

**Tara Singh**

Hi, Priya! I'm Layla Aunty's niece. We've actually met a few times. This party looks AMAZING. Could Priya's Parties plan a party for me and my friends? 🎭

## WHAT I KNOW ABOUT TARA

She is in high school and has lots of friends.

She plays the flute.

She seems really nice.

She loves animals, just like me!

I feel nervous. Planning a party for TEENAGERS will be super-different from planning a party for AUNTIES.

I know what makes aunties happy.

food          comfy places to sit

But I have never been to a teen party. I do not know what teenagers like.

I guess I'll just have to figure it out! So I texted Tara.

Hi, Tara! I'd love to plan your party. Thanks for asking me.

Yay! I love how Priya's Parties raises money for endangered animals! I can't wait to help any animal you pick.

Thank you!!! What kind of party do you want?

It will be a just-for-fun party. It's not my birthday.

I hope Tara writes more soon. I have no idea what a just-for-fun party is . . .

## HOW I'M FEELING

Happy! I get to plan another party!

Nervous! I don't really know what I'm doing.

Worried! What if I disappoint Tara and her friends?

# REAL WORRIES

## Tuesday

I am feeling overwhelmed. Going to school,
helping out with Sammy, AND running a
start-up business is a LOT of work.

Oh! Tara just texted again!

Henna is so pretty! It's a dark brown paste made from henna leaves. People have been using henna for thousands of years to draw designs on their skin. Oh, and henna is also called mehndi (*men-dee*).

comes in
cone-shaped tubes

decorates a bride's hands
and feet

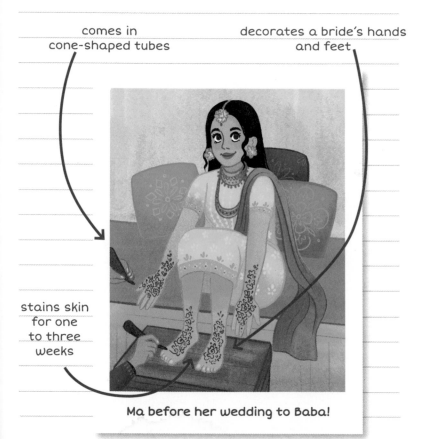

stains skin
for one
to three
weeks

Ma before her wedding to Baba!

11

Melissa likes doing DIY projects. So she helps a lot with Priya's Parties stuff. I asked if she wanted to help with Tara's henna night.

That sounds fun! How can I help?

Great! I'm not sure yet . . .

I'll make a collage tonight. Cutting and pasting different pictures together gives me ideas. I need a party plan ASAP!
(AS SOON AS POSSIBLE)

# PARTY THEMES

Ma invited Layla Aunty for dinner tonight. And Tara came, too.

13

After dinner, we went to my room.

I felt nervous, even though Tara was super-friendly. I had to wipe my hands on my jeans. My palms were sweaty.

We could maybe . . . pick a theme for your party?

Ooh! Good idea!

I'm coming up with party-planning rules to make every party awesome.

## Need for Theme Rule: Pick a great theme.

Henna is a fun activity, but Tara's party still needs a theme to help all the details fit together. A theme creates a vibe.

Bright colors + balloons = happy vibe

Pillows + pizza = cozy vibe

Ghosts + cobwebs = spooky vibe

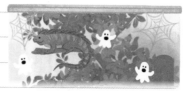

Here's the collage I made last night. I came up with a CLASSIC BOLLYWOOD theme. Most Bollywood movies are love stories. So they have scenes where a bride gets henna before her wedding.

Very colorful!

Always ends the same!
(Happily ever after!)

Super cheesy!

I felt shy about showing my idea to Tara. So first I asked her what she likes . . .

Do you have any favorite colors?

Not really. I like every color. But I don't want rainbows or anything cheesy. I want something UNIQUE.

Okay, so the opposite of a Classic Bollywood theme.

❌ too colorful

❌ too cheesy

❌ totally NOT UNIQUE

YEEKS! Well, my idea was out.

Tara and I needed to brainstorm.

What if we mix two things that do NOT go together? To make a mash-up theme! Like . . . roses and robots.

Or flamingos and . . . wizards!

It could even be a wacky place! Like an underwater jungle!

Ooh!

I know! A galaxy desert! Priya, it's the perfect theme!

Yay! I'll make invitations!

After Tara went home, I made two new collages.

GALAXY

collection of stars

outer space

DESERT

hot sun

cactus

sand

What kind of VIBE will a galaxy-desert party have?

# 4
# PARTY TEAM

## Thursday Morning

Melissa is going to help me get ready for Tara's party. So I let her pick the endangered animal we would help.

# WHY PANGOLINS ARE SPECIAL

There are eight
species of pangolins
in Asia and Africa.

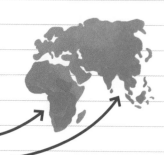

They have very
long tongues. (Helpful
for eating ants!)

Pangolin moms
carry their babies
on their tails.

Pangolins curl into
a ball when they get
scared.

I texted Tara to tell her the party would help pangolins.

Amazing! Just watched videos. I never knew about pangolins before!

I have a lot to do before Saturday.

## Henna Night To-Do List:

 Find someone to do henna.

 Plan and bake a special cake.

 Make galaxy-desert decorations.

The really important part of a henna night is having a henna artist who does amazing designs.

Neda Aunty is an awesome henna artist. So I decided to ask if she could help out.

Hi, Neda Aunty! I'm planning a henna night for Layla Aunty's niece.

Wow, Priya! Your business is really taking off!

Could you be the henna artist at the party?

I'm happy to help!

TWO henna artists sounded better than ONE! So I also asked Padma Aunty to help.

YAY! I can cross one thing off my list.

## Henna Night To-Do List:

♡ ~~Find someone to do henna.~~

♡ Plan and bake a special cake.

♡ Make galaxy-desert decorations.

Oh, and I came up with a top secret idea for Tara's henna design! Padma Aunty and Neda Aunty are going to help me with the surprise.

Okay, I know this is not a birthday party, but every party is better with cake. That should definitely be a party-planning rule.

Sweet Treat Rule:

Serve dessert!

I drew ideas for a special cake.

Here is my plan:

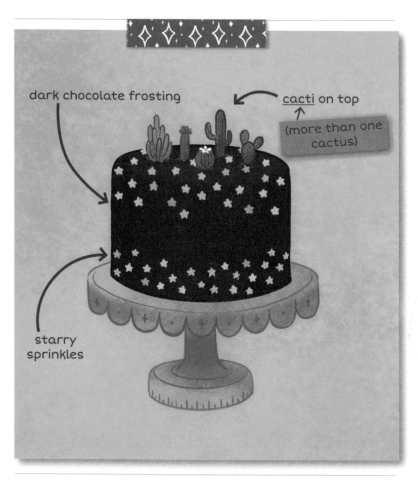

dark chocolate frosting

cacti on top

(more than one cactus)

starry sprinkles

I hope I can make this cake in real life! Now it's time for my hardest brainstorm yet. I have to come up with party decorations for a galaxy-desert theme!

Priya's Parties is all about planning parties that are awesome for the planet! So I like making DIY decorations with recycled materials. (It saves money, too.)

## My Decoration Ideas

⭐ Cardboard cacti

⭐ Glittery stars

⭐ Starry lanterns

# Here are the craft supplies I gathered:

⭐ Cardboard and paper

⭐ Markers

⭐ Glitter — Earth-safe!

⭐ Scissors

⭐ Empty cans

I filled five cans with water and put them in the freezer!

⭐ Hammer and nails

Can I get everything done before Saturday?

# TOO MUCH SPARKLE

## Thursday Afternoon

Tara texted me her party invitation. She designed it herself!

You are invited to Tara's
**GALAXY-DESERT
HENNA NIGHT!**
Hosted by
**Priya's Parties**
to help save pangolins!
Saturday
5:00 p.m.

Wow! You made this invitation? It looks super-GREAT!

Thanks, Priya! I'll send it to everyone now!

I love making art on my computer. I want to be a graphic designer someday.

I have to do a super-GREAT job for Tara now.

Melissa came over after school to help make the decorations.

I hope Melissa is right. I really don't want to let Tara down.

We decided to take a break from making stars. Melissa and I picked four strange and amazing cacti to paint!

## COOL CACTI

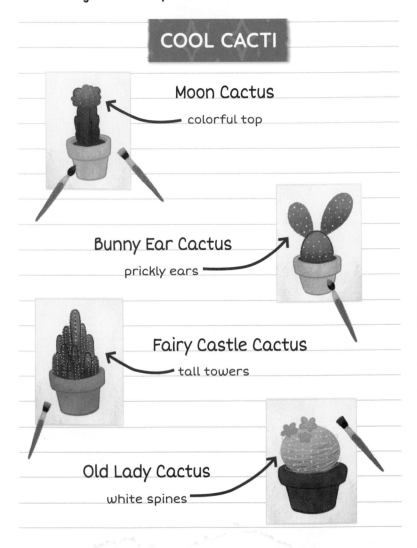

### Moon Cactus
colorful top

### Bunny Ear Cactus
prickly ears

### Fairy Castle Cactus
tall towers

### Old Lady Cactus
white spines

I went to check on the cans I'd put in the freezer. Melissa and Sammy followed me.

We took out all five cans.

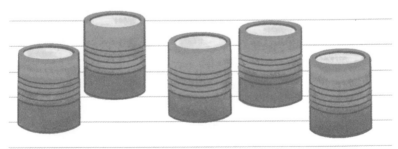

I showed Melissa what to do.

I asked Ma to help us hammer nails to punch holes in the cans.

Next, we ran the cold cans under hot water
until the ice chunks slid out.

I can't wait to see what we made!

Finally, it was time for the big test! Melissa
put a candle inside one can. Ma lit it. Then I
turned off the lights . . .

The candlelight made a starry pattern on the table.

That's beautiful.

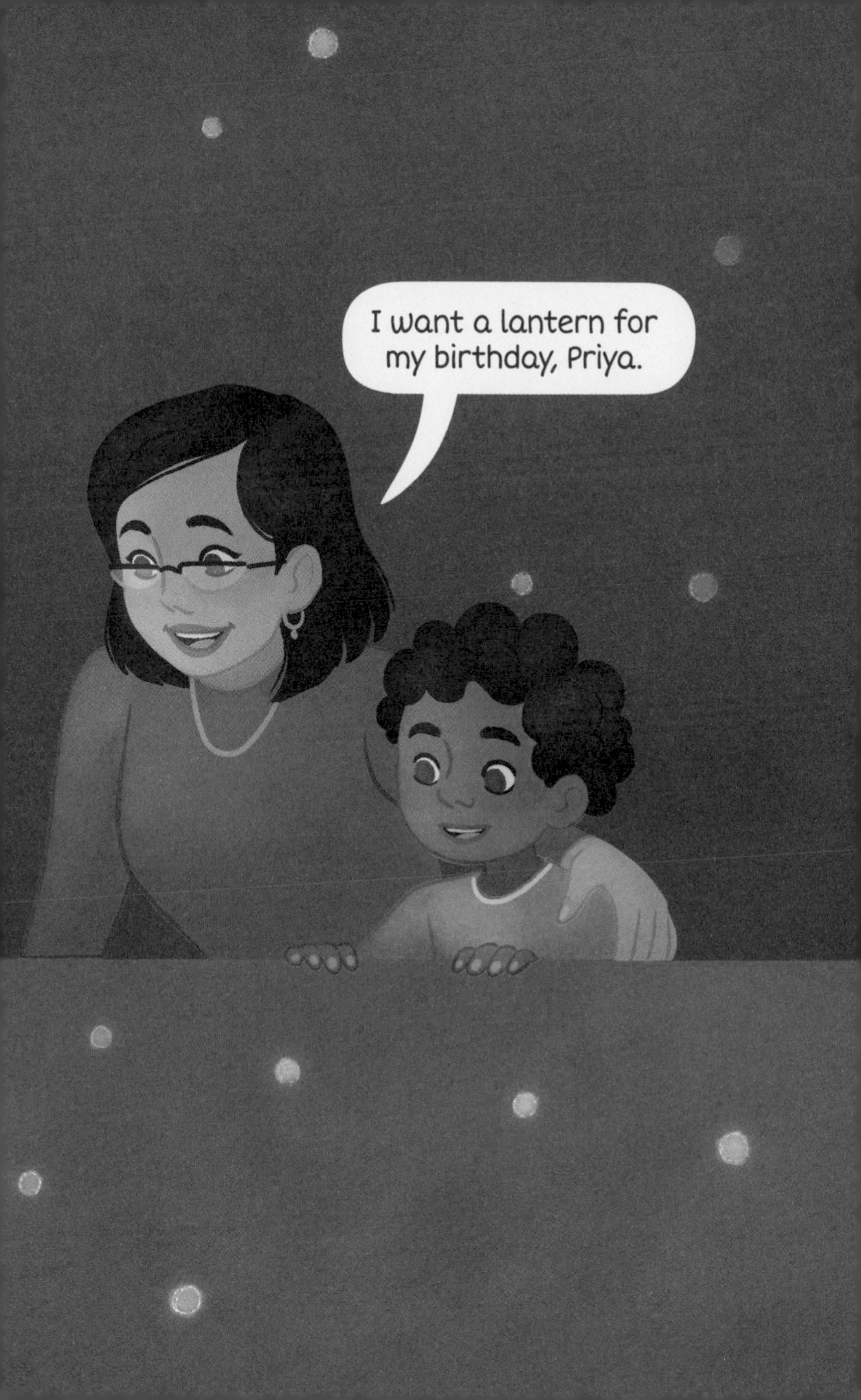
I want a lantern for my birthday, Priya.

Melissa had to go home.

I need to practice my dance routine.
I keep mixing up the steps.

You'll get it! Thanks for
your help!

I had to finish a ZILLION more stars.
Sammy still wanted to help, but sometimes his
help makes more work for me.

Don't shake the glitter!
It'll explode everywhere.

The glitter EXPLODED everywhere.

Baba saw the mess and took a deep breath. It looked like a group of WILD FAIRIES had thrown a party in my room.

Being a CEO in charge of your own business is really hard. (Chief Executive Officer = The Big Boss with Lots of Responsibilities)

# PARTY PREP

Today at school, Ethan Jackman made fun of me.

My ears felt hot. I showered last night, but I guess glitter was hiding in my hair!

At lunch, Melissa and Dola tried cheering me up.

Priya, I love how you sparkle.

Want to see some cute pangolin photos? Their scales are like armor!

The rest of the day, I pretended to have pangolin armor. Pangolin scales are so tough, even a lion can't chew through them.

I biked home with Melissa.

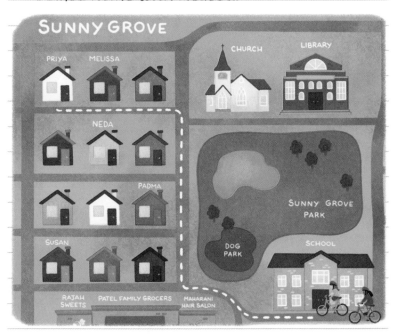

I was actually happy when Sammy asked me to read his dinosaur book again. It felt really comforting.

Now I have to get down to business, though.

I finished the stars. They look supergood, but they are shedding glitter EVERYWHERE. Baba will have to take LOTS of deep breaths when he walks around the house!

Maybe Priya's Parties won't use glitter after this. It is VERY hard to clean up.

Dida and I worked on my cake idea. I love being in the kitchen with Dida. We talk about all sorts of things!

What is your favorite memory from growing up in India?

All the festivals. They were always full of fun and family.

SUGAR

The cake turned out a little crooked, but I'm going to cover it with frosting and sprinkles.

This cake isn't the best. I'm glad I also planned a henna surprise for Tara.

You fixed the cake very nicely, Priya. Too much chocolate for me, though.

I flopped onto my bed and stared up at the ceiling.

What if Tara doesn't like chocolate?

What if a guest is allergic to eggs? I should have checked!

Should I even bring my wonky cake?

It's too late to change anything since the party is tomorrow! I just hope it turns out okay.

# SETTING UP

Neda Aunty drove Padma Aunty and me to Tara's house two hours before the party. I had to SQUISH in next to boxes full of party stuff.

We brought all the henna supplies.

And it looks like you brought everything else, Priya!

henna cones

lemons
(Lemon juice makes the
henna darker!)

mehndi
designs
binder

Tara helped us carry the boxes in from the car. My palms started sweating.

Her house was really nice inside. There was a big, twisty staircase and a chandelier in the entryway.

I felt embarrassed, because maybe Tara thought I was trying too hard. I don't know why that would be a BAD thing, but my whole face got warm.

Tara had set out bowls
with rocks and succulents
(suhk-yuh-luhnts) in them.
Succulents can grow in
dry places. Unlike cacti,
they have big, juicy leaves
that store water!

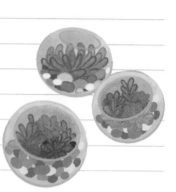

Tara helped
me hang the wall
decorations.

What's in there?

Oh, that's for later. No peeking!

As a final touch, we set out the starry lanterns. Then Tara dimmed the lights.

Wow, Priya! It looks like a magical galaxy in here!

But we can't do henna in the dark!

Okay . . . We need half galaxy, half desert.

I turned half the lights back on. Now the room really looked like a galaxy-desert!

Tara's party food looked like a work of art.
I also helped her make fancy water with lime,
lemon, and mint.

The clock said 5:07 p.m., which was seven
minutes AFTER the party was supposed to
start. Where was everyone?

# AWESOME PLAYLIST

## Saturday Late Afternoon

Finally, the doorbell rang. All the guests arrived at the same time! Do teenagers like doing everything together?

58

The party started.

Bex and Mishka were getting henna done.

Eddie and Sofia looked through the designs binder.

Tara poured drinks. Lauren took pictures. I took pictures, too.

But the VIBE didn't feel right . . .

Everybody was too quiet. So I came up with another rule for an awesome party!

## Soundtrack for Success Rule: Have a great playlist.

Good music can change the energy of a party.

Gentle classical music = calm, peaceful party

Loud rock music = jump-around dance party

Happy pop music = toddler party

I thought people had forgotten I was in the room, so I felt shy about speaking up. But I knew it was my responsibility to make sure the party was awesome.

Let's make a party playlist . . .
Everyone can add songs.

Ooh! Great idea!

I've got a good song!

Once the music started, it was like MAGIC. People relaxed. They started talking and laughing. It felt like I was in a movie about an awesome party.

Now felt like a good time to reveal the cake.

I made a galaxy <u>dessert</u>!

Oh my gosh!

Tara said it was time for a couple of surprises before she got her henna done. My stomach did a flip. I like GIVING surprises, but I don't like GETTING surprises. They totally stress me out!

# SURPRISES

## 9

## Saturday Evening

SURPRISE #1: Tara gave me a card that everybody had signed.

Thank you for organizing a henna night!

We made a donation to save pangolins on behalf of Priya's Parties.

Tara  Sofia  Eddie  Mishka
Lauren  Bex

SURPRISE #2: Tara gave me a small box.
Inside there were lots of cards.

They're <u>business cards</u>!
I made them for you.
Thanks for planning this
amazing party.

I took out one card.

**Priya's Parties**

HELPING THE PLANET ONE AWESOME PARTY AT A TIME!

**Priya Chakraborty**
Founder and CEO

I blinked a lot, because I did NOT want to cry
in front of teenagers. I felt overwhelmed—in a
good way, though.

Next, Neda Aunty and Padma Aunty worked on Tara's henna.

Then I announced the henna surprise.

There are six hidden pictures in Tara's mehndi! See if you can find them all!

Oh my gosh! This is so special, Priya. Thank you!

🌵 Cactus     🪐 Saturn

🐾 Pangolin     ☄️ Comet

🌞 Sun     ⭐ Star

Starry Galaxy-Desert-Pangolin Henna Night was a big success. Everything worked out! I even got my henna done, too. I was smiling the whole way home.

There was one more surprise for the day . . .

Sammy finally picked a different book to read before bed! It was about dragons.

# NEXT UP

## 10

**Sunday**

Melissa and I ate cake for breakfast today. I'd saved two slices from the party! I also showed Melissa my new business cards.

Tara gave me this succulent. I thought Harry might like it. It's safe for reptiles.

Ooh, thanks! I'll put it in his terrarium.

Melissa and I chose the best party pictures to post.

Priya Chakraborty

Tara's Starry Henna Night was
**OUT OF THIS WORLD.**

**Eddie Lu**

Last night was unbelievable! #partywithpriya

**Tara Singh**

I can't stop staring at my henna! That party was the most fun party ever. Thanks, Priya!

**Lauren Garcia**

STELLAR party! Everybody has been asking where I got my mehndi.

**Reeta Chakraborty**

So proud of you, Priya! Can you plan an anniversary party for me and your dad? (He never checks here. Let's keep it a secret, okay?) Love, Ma

Ooh! A secret party for my parents! Sounds tricky and exciting!

# DIY YOUR PARTY!
# STARRY LANTERN

Recycle a can into a punched-hole lantern.

## WHAT YOU'LL NEED

- Paper
- Scissors
- Empty can (clean, with all labels removed)
- Pencil
- Tape

- Safety glasses
- Towel
- Hammer and one nail (or an electric drill)
- Small candle

## GET STARTED

1. Measure and cut paper to fit around the can.

2. Fill the can with water and put it in the freezer overnight. (The ice will keep the can from denting when you punch the holes.)

3. Draw a dot design on your paper to guide where you will punch holes. Make sure the dots are at least ¼-inch apart.

4. Take the can out of the freezer. Wrap the paper around the can full of ice. Tape your design in place.

*For steps 5-6, work with an adult and wear safety glasses to protect your eyes.*

5. Lay the frozen can on a folded towel so it 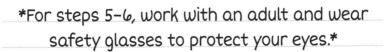 doesn't roll. Choose one dot in your design to start with. Then hammer (or drill) a hole into the dot on the can. Remove the nail (or drill). Repeat for all the dots in your pattern.

6. Run hot tap water over the can until the ice block pops out. Then dry off the can. (Be careful around the punched holes!)

7. Place a small candle inside your lantern.

## PARTY TIME

Enjoy the pretty pattern of lights at your party!

Find two times when things don't turn out quite right and/or Priya has to change plans. (If needed, look back at pages 17, 48, and 59.)

 Priya shares four facts about pangolins on page 21. Do some research! Can you come up with two new facts?

 Priya makes three DIY decorations for the party. List them. Then come up with another galaxy-desert-themed decoration idea.

 Priya does not like surprises, but she receives a few super ones in this book. What are the three surprises? (If needed, reread Chapter 9.)

 One of Priya's rules for an awesome party is to have a great playlist. Make your own party playlist! What songs would you include?

# ABOUT THE CREATORS

**Mitali Banerjee Ruths** grew up in Texas and was a LOT like Priya when she was younger. She wanted to start a business, save the planet, and help endangered animals.

Mitali now lives in Canada. She still cares about animals, protecting the environment, and finding ways to be a better earthling. Sometimes when she gets scared or worried, Mitali curls into a ball like a pangolin.

**Aaliya Jaleel** loves illustrating books with bright, bold color palettes and exciting, lovable characters. When she is not drawing, she's planning fun parties that never quite go as planned—but that turn out memorable nonetheless.

Aaliya currently lives in Texas with her husband. She loves exploring and finding hidden treasures when traveling to new places.

# The Party Diaries

## Read more books!

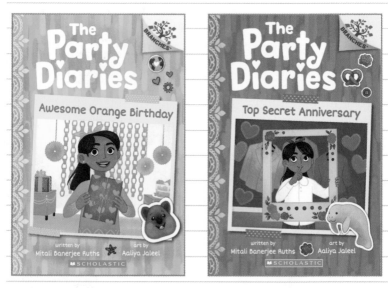

The Party Diaries

**Awesome Orange Birthday**

written by
Mitali Banerjee Ruths

art by
Aaliya Jaleel

**SCHOLASTIC**

The Party Diaries

**Top Secret Anniversary**

written by
Mitali Banerjee Ruths

art by
Aaliya Jaleel

**SCHOLASTIC**